Hey, kids!
See if you can spot Santa,
Mrs. Claus, and Reindeer
hidden throughout the story.

To...

You made it onto Santa's NICE list—GOOD JOB!

MERRY CHRISTMAS!

Love, from..

I SAW SANTA IN
SOUTH DAKOTA

Written by J.D. Green

Illustrated by Nadja Sarell and Srimalie Bassani

 sourcebooks
jabberwocky

anta's not planned his vacation this year.
Mrs. Claus says, "How 'bout South Dakota, my dear?
You always say it's your favorite place,
but remember, the children should not see your face."

"It's true," Santa says. "South Dakota has it all:
great sights, tasty bites, fun times great and small."

Mrs. Claus says, "We should set off tonight!
And you heard what I said? You must keep out of sight!"

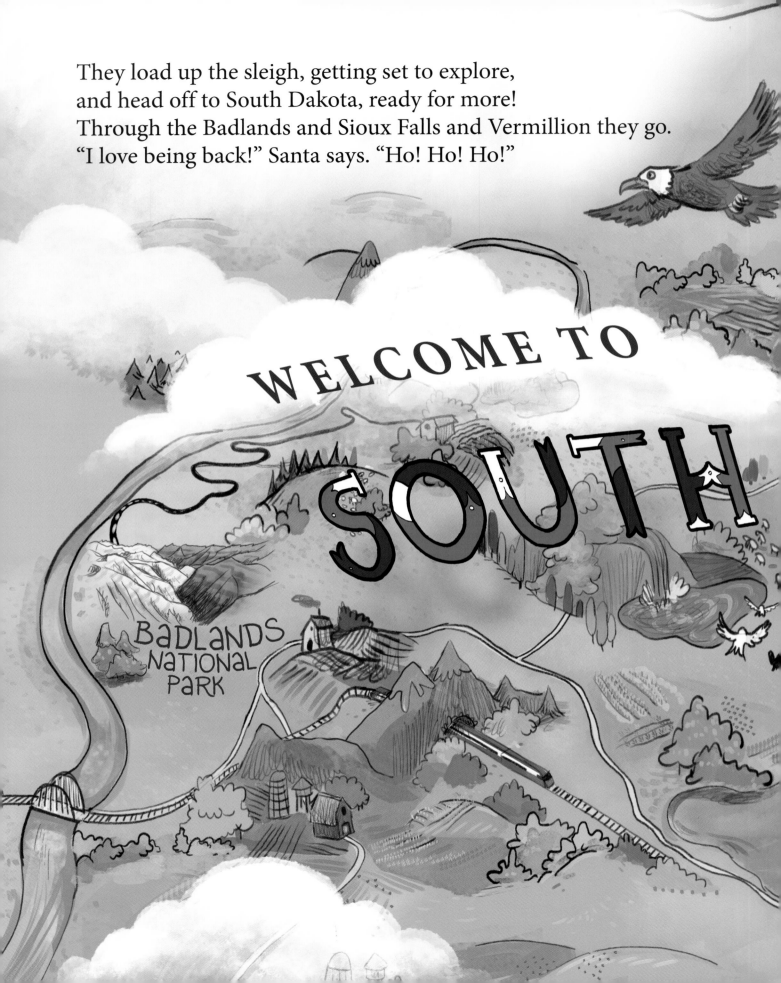

They load up the sleigh, getting set to explore,
and head off to South Dakota, ready for more!
Through the Badlands and Sioux Falls and Vermillion they go.
"I love being back!" Santa says. "Ho! Ho! Ho!"

WELCOME TO SOUTH

BADLANDS NATIONAL PARK

It's a family tradition, when they go away,
to buy a few gifts to remember their stay.

Smart Mrs. Claus came prepared with a list,
so first she'll go shop—not one friend will be missed!

Santa thinks buying nice gifts is quite tough.
He's feeling confused—there's just so much stuff!

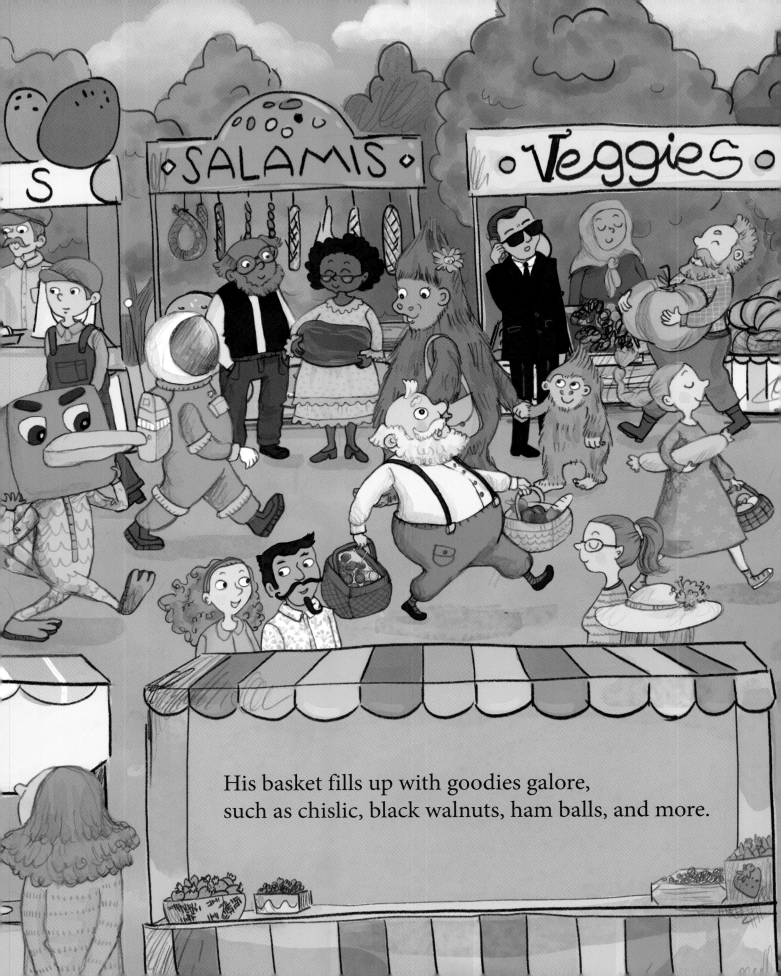

His basket fills up with goodies galore,
such as chislic, black walnuts, ham balls, and more.

Reindeer's not eager to stick to plans,
there's so much to see and experience firsthand!

But first he must find a good new disguise,
so he can blend in with the crowd outside!

The Clauses are done with their shopping for friends.
Now it's time to go sightseeing before their trip ends!

Back in the North Pole, Head Elf checks the mail.
He opens one letter and turns very pale…

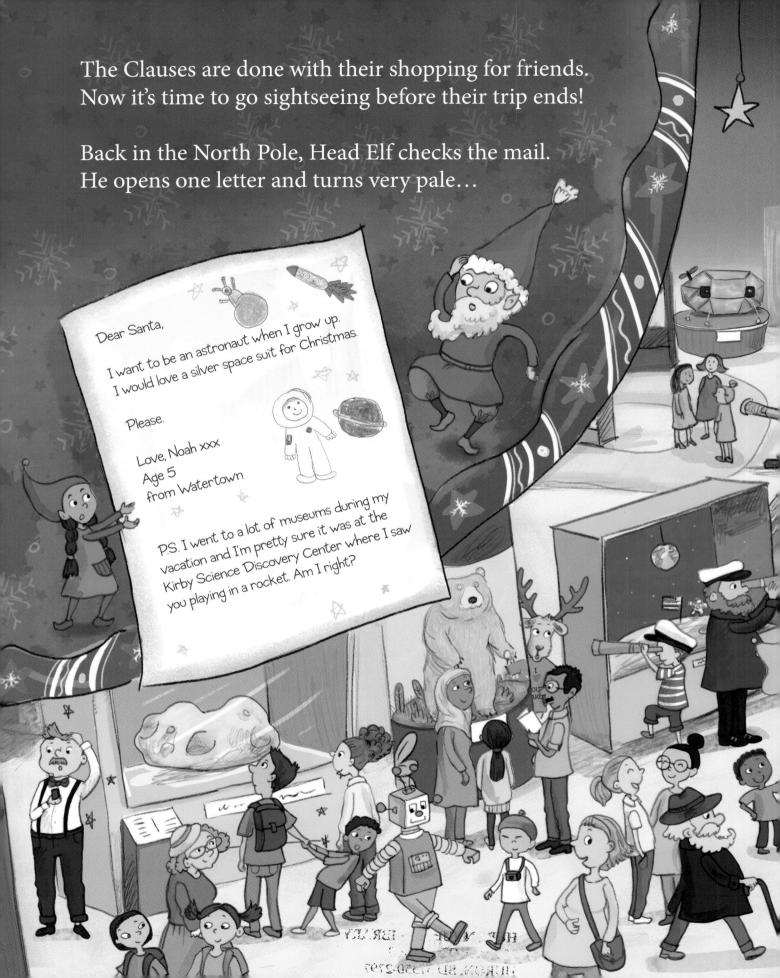

Dear Santa,

I want to be an astronaut when I grow up.
I would love a silver space suit for Christmas.

Please.

Love, Noah xxx
Age 5
from Watertown

P.S. I went to a lot of museums during my vacation and I'm pretty sure it was at the Kirby Science Discovery Center where I saw you playing in a rocket. Am I right?

Dear Santa,

My favorite place in the whole wide world is the ocean! Please can I have a snorkel and flippers for Christmas? Thank you!

By the way, I was at WaTiki Indoor Waterpark Resort yesterday. I didn't have my glasses on while I was swimming, but I saw someone with a big, white beard and a red-and-white bathing suit. Was it you? Please write back and tell me.

Love, Emma
Age 7
from Mobridge

At home in the North, Head Elf says, "This won't do! One sighting is terrible. Now we've had two!"

Santa should really be taking more care.
It seems yet more children have spotted him there.

Dear Santa,

I would love, love, love a big, pink unicorn!
I drew one for you here.

Love, Bella x X x
Age 5¾
from Brandon

P.S. Did I see you at Newton Hills State Park,
wearing green hiking boots and a red-and-white
striped backpack? It even sounded like you were
whistling "Hail, South Dakota."

Am I right?

Reading the mail, Head Elf shakes his head.
This letter has caused him to turn slightly red!

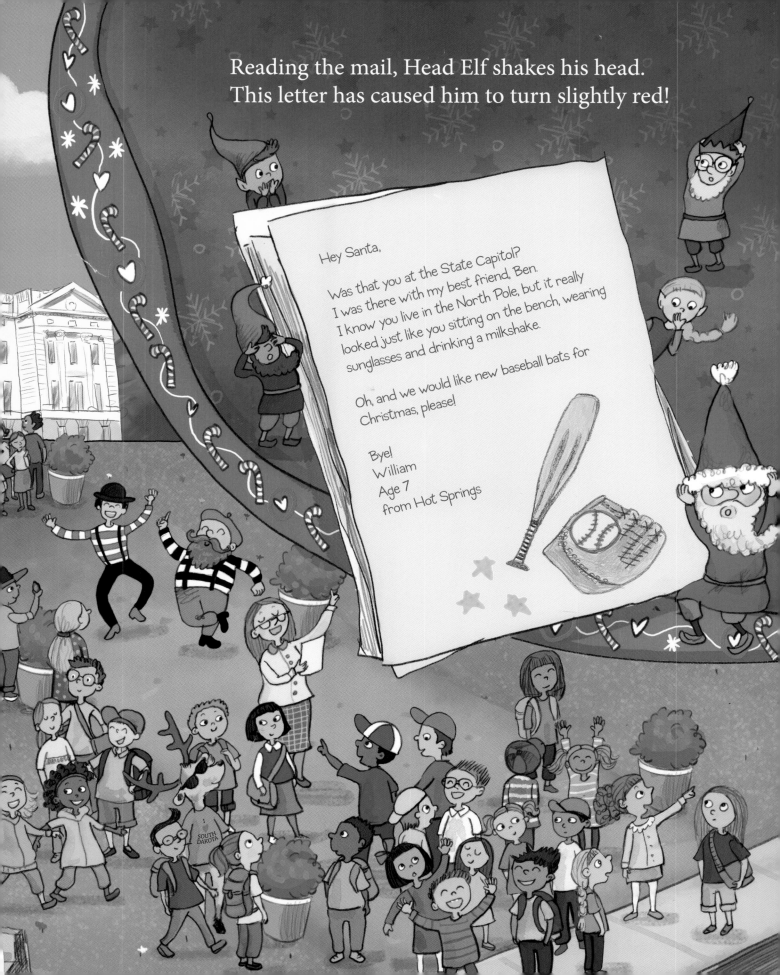

Hey Santa,

Was that you at the State Capitol?
I was there with my best friend, Ben.
I know you live in the North Pole, but it really
looked just like you sitting on the bench, wearing
sunglasses and drinking a milkshake.

Oh, and we would like new baseball bats for
Christmas, please!

Bye!
William
Age 7
from Hot Springs

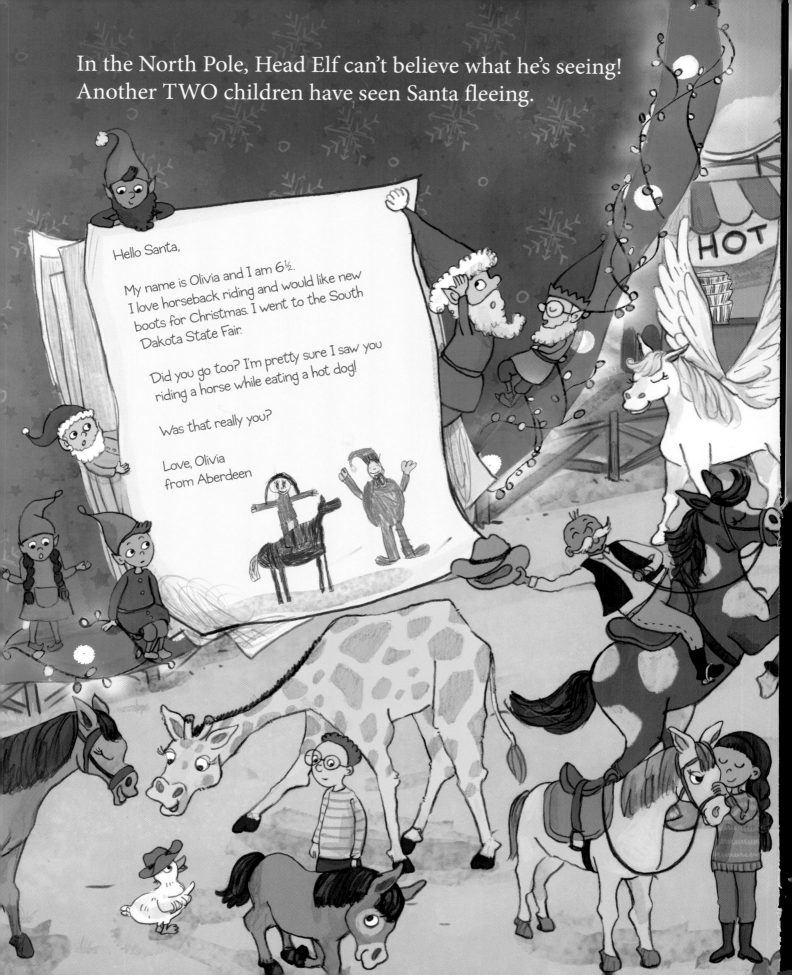

In the North Pole, Head Elf can't believe what he's seeing!
Another TWO children have seen Santa fleeing.

Hello Santa,

My name is Olivia and I am 6½.
I love horseback riding and would like new
boots for Christmas. I went to the South
Dakota State Fair.

Did you go too? I'm pretty sure I saw you
riding a horse while eating a hot dog!

Was that really you?

Love, Olivia
from Aberdeen

HOT

Hi Santa,

I am 8 and I would like a real duck for Christmas. My grandpa and I were watching the ducks at Canyon Lake Park when we saw a big, red sleigh on the other side of the pond. I heard the park ranger say sleighs do not float.

Was that you?

James
from Spearfish

The vacation is over; the shopping is done.
See you soon, South Dakota! Thanks for the fun!

Upon arriving home, Head Elf lets Santa know he's been spotted by multiple children. Oh no!

Emma, age 7

Noah, age 5

Dear Noah,
Yes, you did spot me at the museum! I was on my summer vacation in South Dakota.

Enjoy your silver space suit.

Love, Santa
x

Dear Emma,
Yes, you did spot me at WaTiki Indoor Waterpark Resort! South Dakota is my favorite place to visit.

Have fun with your snorkel and flippers.

Love, Santa
x

Bella, age 5¾

Dear Bella,
Yes, you did spot me at Newton Hills State Park! I was on my summer vacation in South Dakota.

Have fun with your pink unicorn!

Love, Santa
x

Mrs. Claus and Santa know just what to do.
They'll clean up this mess with a special gift or two.

Olivia, age 6½

Dear Olivia,
Yes, I was riding a horse at the South Dakota State Fair this summer! South Dakota is my favorite place to visit.
Enjoy your new boots!
Love, Santa
x

William, age 7

Dear William,
You sure did spot me at the State Capitol! I was on my summer vacation in South Dakota.
Hope you like your new baseball bat!
Love, Santa
x

James, age 8

Dear James,
Yes, you did spot me at Canyon Lake Park! I love visiting South Dakota on my summer vacation.
Have fun playing with your real duck!
Love, Santa
x

When Christmas arrives, all the children who wrote get one EXTRA gift, and inside is a note…

To my favorite child in South Dakota,

On my summer break, I like getting away,
so I go to South Dakota, the best place to stay.
There's so much in South Dakota that I like to see,
there really is no place that I'd rather be.

So be on the lookout, 'cuz you never know,
if I might be somewhere that you like to go.
And if you have time, I like nothing better
than hearing from YOU! So write me a letter!

Merry Christmas!

Love,

Santa

xxx

Written by J.D. Green
Illustrated by Nadja Sarell and Srimalie Bassani
Additional art by Jerry Pyke and Darran Holmes
Designed by Geff Newland

Published by Sourcebooks Jabberwocky, an imprint of Sourcebooks, Inc.
P.O. Box 4410, Naperville, Illinois 60567-4410
(630) 961-3900
Fax: (630) 961-2168
jabberwockykids.com

Date of Production: August 2018
Run Number: HTW_PO201802
Printed and bound in China (GD)
10 9 8 7 6 5 4 3 2 1

Hey, kids! Flick back and see if you can spot Santa,
Mrs. Claus, and Reindeer hidden throughout the story.